THE CONTEST
00:00:05

TURN THE TABLES

Megan Atwood

D1359456

Copyright © 2016 by Megan Atwood

All rights reserved. International copyright secured. No part of this book may be reproduced, stored in a retrieval system, or transmitted in any form or by any means—electronic, mechanical, photocopying, recording, or otherwise—without the prior written permission of Lerner Publishing Group, Inc., except for the inclusion of brief quotations in an acknowledged review.

Darby Creek
A division of Lerner Publishing Group, Inc.
241 First Avenue North
Minneapolis, MN 55401 USA

For reading levels and more information, look up this title at
www.lernerbooks.com.

The images in this book are used with the permission of: © Andycash/Dreamstime. com (digital clock); © Vidakovic/Bigstock.com (Abstract technology background); © iStockphoto.com/archibald1221 (circle background): © freesoulproduction/ Shutterstock.com (game pieces). © iStockphoto.com/Kubrak78 (city skyline); Teens from Top to Bottom: © Amy Dunn/Dreamstime.com; © iStockphoto.com/ hartcreations; © iStockphoto.com/TomFullum; © g-stockstudio/Shutterstock.com.

Main body text set in Janson Text LT Std 12/17.5.
Typeface provided by Adobe Systems.

Library of Congress Cataloging-in-Publication Data

The Cataloging-in-Publication Data for *Turn the Tables* is on file at the Library of Congress.
ISBN 978-1-4677-7510-6 (lib. bdg.)
ISBN 978-1-4677-8105-3 (pbk.)
ISBN 978-1-4677-8835-9 (EB pdf)

Manufactured in the United States of America
1 – SB – 12/31/15

To my parents, always.

CHAPTER 1

JAMES

Everything the Benefactor told you is a lie.

James stared at the words that Ana had typed on her tablet. This had to be a mistake. He'd done everything the Benefactor told him to. All ten tasks, with the promise of $10 million if he finished the Contest before the other three contestants.

Some of those tasks had made him shudder, but there *had* to be a payoff. James needed this Contest to be real.

But Ana went on: *This guy is dangerous. He's forced us to do all kinds of illegal stuff. And once we were in, he made sure none of us could back out. He threatened us and the people we loved. Whoever this person is, we need to find out and stop them.*

James reached for the tablet. They had to pass it back and forth to type messages to each other, because all four contestants—James, Ana, Maiv, and Colin—were keeping silent. They'd agreed not to talk while they were in the van, since it was probably bugged. By the Benefactor. The creator of the Contest.

James tapped out on the touchscreen keys: *My grandpa's really sick. I need the prize money to pay for his treatment.*

Ana looked up at him with a mixture of surprise and sympathy. Then she shook her head and wrote, *There is no prize money.*

James clenched his teeth and looked out the window. On some level, he'd known that. He'd known he was being used and that the Benefactor wasn't legit. But he'd wanted so desperately to believe . . .

The nightmare he'd been living was for nothing. And here he was, with his family thinking he'd run away, a pawn in someone else's game. But worst of all: His grandpa would not be helped. He would die.

James tried hard to hold the tears in as he watched the streetlights pass by, one after another. The streets of downtown Minneapolis were empty this late at night. He felt empty too—empty of hope, empty of energy.

He felt a tap on his shoulder. Ana had written more. *He's not planning to let any of us "win." His plan is to get what he needs from us and then kill us.*

Now James turned completely toward Ana, his eyes wide. He wrote: *You can't be serious.*

Ana's hands flew over the screen. *All along, he's just been using us. Once he doesn't need us to do his dirty work anymore, he'll want to cover his tracks. In case we try to tell someone what we know.*

James couldn't wrap his head around this. No prize money. No life-saving treatment for his grandpa. And now this: death. The brush with the security guard at SolarStar was still trembling through him. That had been a close call. He wasn't ready for a closer one.

Maiv, the girl in the front passenger's seat, gestured at Colin, the tall white guy who was driving the van. Colin slowed down and pulled over.

James had met Ana a few days earlier—sort of—and a few minutes ago she had told him Colin and Maiv's names when he'd typed out *Who are these people?* Tonight wasn't the night for formal introductions.

Up until now, James had thought these people were his enemies. Or at least people to beat—enemies was too strong a word. Still, all of a sudden, he realized they might be his only chance to get out of this mess.

Colin shut off the engine. The sudden quiet freaked James out even more. He and the other three got out fast. They stood in a circle on the sidewalk.

Maiv started. "They're going to try to kill us tonight. That's their only move now. And if we call the police, we'll just get arrested. No one will believe the Contest is real. So we have to make a choice. Do we try to get away somehow? Or do we go and meet them now, on our own terms?"

"What do you mean by *on our own terms*?"

James asked. That option didn't sound very safe.

Maiv raised her chin so she could look him in the eye. James could practically feel her resolve. "I mean we take them down."

"How?" Colin pressed. The guy was clearly on edge—not as confident as Maiv.

"Well, I have an idea," Maiv said. "Look, the Benefactor is dangerous. We know that. You don't mastermind something as complicated as this unless you have some real evil in your heart, some need for control. But I think we can take advantage of that. If you guys will trust me, I think we can find a way to prove that he's behind this—and stop him from hurting anyone else. What do you say?"

James looked from Ana to Colin and finally back to Maiv. She seemed super on top of everything, really determined. His grandpa used to say about his wife, James's grandma, "I'd follow that woman through a wall of fire if she thought it was a good idea. She was that smart."

James thought he knew what his grandpa had meant.

Ana broke the silence. "I don't know you at

all. I don't know what you have in mind. But no way am I letting this Benefactor get the best of me. No way."

Colin nodded. "Same with me."

James took a deep breath. "After the night I've had—the *week* I've had—yeah, I'm open to anything."

"Good," said Maiv. "Then let's take this guy down. First step, go to the river and see who's waiting for us."

"I thought you said you already know who the Benefactor is," Ana said, her eyebrows furrowed. "Why would we walk straight into their trap?"

"I don't think the Benefactor will go to the river in person," Maiv explained, tucking her hair behind her ears. "I don't think he plans to kill us himself. Just like I don't think he's been sneaking around our houses and schools planting bugs himself. He's got someone working for him—maybe a bunch of people."

James groaned out loud. "Great. This just gets more and more complicated."

Maiv shot him a sympathetic look. "Well,

not really. Our choice is still simple. Try to run, knowing the Benefactor and his spies will probably catch us—or go to the river and try to get some answers from whoever is there."

Colin looked doubtful. "Try to get some answers from the person who's waiting to kill us?"

"Yes," said Maiv. And then she pulled out a gun.

CHAPTER 2

MAIV

"I took this out of the trash," Maiv told James and Ana, who were gaping at her. "Thought it might come in handy. They don't have to know it's empty."

"So that's the gun I left under the bench for James," said Ana. "The one he was supposed to bring into SolarStar."

"Yeah," said Colin. "Maiv realized James had thrown it away. She went back for it while you two were in the building."

James let out his breath in a *whoosh*. "Man, for a second I thought you were about to kill us," he said to Maiv.

Maiv smiled. "Nope, I'm on your side."

Colin said, "I hate to even use an empty gun."

"But considering who we're dealing with, it may not hurt to have it," Ana said, her eyebrow raised.

"Right," said Maiv. "So we're agreed?"

The others nodded.

"Let's get going."

* * *

The van turned onto a narrow road that snaked right by the river. It was overrun with trees and smattered with little parks here and there.

In the darkness, the van's headlights lit up the water on one side and the woods on the other but not much else. "I think that's the park up ahead," said Colin, nodding toward a clearing in the trees. A small parking area lay just off the road, with one car waiting there.

Maiv motioned for Colin to keep driving. Then, about fifty yards farther down the road, she gestured for him to pull over. He parked along the side of the road, and they all got out.

Maiv whispered, "OK. Here's what I think

we should do. Three of us will go meet whoever it is. "James, you've got the folder with the schematics? Good. We're supposed to be giving them those. We'll say the fourth person decided not to come. We'll keep them distracted while the fourth person sneaks around and then surprises them. Is everyone cool with that?"

"I assume the fourth person will be the one with the gun?" said Colin.

Maiv shrugged. "Seems like that would make the most sense."

"I'll do it," Ana said.

"You sure?" said James. "I could do it. I owe you, for helping me out back at SolarStar."

"It's fine, I want to do it," Ana insisted.

Maiv nodded. "Good. I think that'll be more of a surprise. Remember, we don't want to hurt this person—just get information. And make sure they don't hurt us."

"Yeah, no sweat," said Colin dryly.

* * *

Walking through the dead leaves on the side of the road, Maiv felt like an elephant trampling over bubble wrap. She hoped the group wasn't making as much noise as she thought they were. She didn't let herself look back to see where Ana was.

"Don't let me pass out," she heard James whisper to Colin.

"Don't *let* you pass out?" Colin whispered back. "No guarantees, man. That's kind of up to you."

"Yeah, but like, catch me if I do?" He laughed a little.

Maiv heard Colin laugh back. She was glad for the little bit of fun they could eke out of this horrible situation. He said to James, "I'll do my best. Now you have to promise to do the same for me too."

By now they had reached the parking lot. The butterflies in Maiv's stomach multiplied. This was it. Maiv watched as a door in the car opened and a man stepped out. Out of the corner of her eyes, Maiv saw James shift the file folder from hand to hand.

A short, compact man stepped away from the car. Maiv couldn't see him very well, but she could tell he was wearing jeans, some pretty hip shoes for an old guy, and a black jacket that clung to him. Maiv hoped that meant there was no weapon hidden underneath.

"Stop right there," the guy said.

The three of them stood shoulder to shoulder, facing him.

"There are supposed to be four of you."

Maiv cleared her throat and said, "The other girl decided not to come. She was too freaked out."

"Did you bring the file?" the guy asked.

James held up the file. Maiv noticed that his arm shook.

The guy breathed out a long sigh. "Thank God. I hope that means this is over."

His voice was starting to sound familiar . . . In fact, not just his voice, but the way he stood . . . Maiv squinted at him, trying to see his face in the darkness.

"So who won?" Colin asked. "One of us is supposed to get a check, right? So who is it?"

The guy shook his head. "I . . . I can't answer that."

"Aren't you part of the Contest?" Colin

went on. "Don't you know who gets the $10 million?"

"I'm really—not supposed to say anything."

Suddenly James blurted out, "I know you."

"No, I don't think so."

"You're Paul," said James. "You have a wife and two kids, and you live in a nice house in St. Paul."

It clicked for Maiv too. The phone call, the person who had followed her. "Paul Grayson," she added. "You used to work for EarthWatch."

"Shut up!" With that, Paul whipped out a gun and pointed it shakily at the three of them. "Don't come any closer, and don't say anything else."

Maiv wondered where Ana was.

"You're not working for the Benefactor." James sounded amazingly calm, though Maiv could tell his eyes were locked on the gun. "I followed you around the other day, and left you a threatening message. Remember that? I didn't do it for fun, and I know it wasn't fun for you either."

Maiv admired James for doing that. Great idea—letting Paul know they were all on the same side. She jumped in. "The Benefactor's blackmailing you, isn't he?"

Paul's voice was shaky but he held the gun steady. "I've never heard of anyone called the Benefactor."

"But *someone's* blackmailing you," Maiv said, taking a step closer.

Paul shook his head. Not as if he was denying it. More like he was refusing to hear the question. "It's almost over. We'll all be done with this soon. So just—stop—asking —questions."

That's when Ana came out from behind the car and stuck the gun in his back. Maiv heard her say, "Drop it."

Paul immediately set the gun on the ground.

Ana said, "Kick it away from yourself but to the right." *Smart*, thought Maiv. Kicking a loaded gun might discharge it. Ana was making sure they wouldn't be in the path of a bullet.

Paul put his hands up and kicked the gun. It skidded across the cement, landing about five feet to the left of Colin. Colin moved to stand over it but didn't pick it up.

Ana kept the empty gun leveled at Paul. "I'm afraid we're not done asking questions."

The guy seemed to deflate. "Listen. I don't know anything. I don't know who they are, or how they know so much about me. But they threatened my family. I can't back out of this. And I can't help you. Someone's on the way to meet us right now, and then it'll all be over."

"Oh man," said Colin. "This guy isn't here to kill us, is he? The main act hasn't shown up yet."

"Apparently not." Maiv sized Paul up. Other than pulling a gun on them—which, to be fair, they'd also done to him—he mostly just seemed scared and confused, like them. "I think he's here for the same reason we are. Because the Benefactor told him to show up. And yeah, I think someone is on the way to kill all five of us."

Paul gaped at them. "Did you say *kill us*?"

Ana sighed and lowered the gun. "Yeah. Whoever you're working for doesn't want any loose ends. Looks like you're another loose end, Paul, so we may be in the same boat. Want to tell us how that happened?"

"I told you, I don't know anything! I got contacted out of the blue by someone who knew—stuff about me. I'm not getting into it, just—stuff that could ruin my life, if people found out. And then the threats, and—I just went along with everything, I had no choice."

"And what exactly was everything?" Maiv pressed. "What did he ask you to do?"

"He wanted information about EarthWatch. About who worked there, how things were set up. And he had me follow people—some of you. And make strange phone calls and leave notes for people." He took a deep breath. "And then he told me to bring this gun to this spot at this time, and said that would be the last thing I needed to do for him."

"Uh-huh," said Ana flatly. "And it didn't seem like a bad idea to you."

"I didn't have another option!"

That's when Maiv saw the headlights. "Here's another option," she said. "Let's get out of here before the real assassin shows up and we *all* die."

Before anyone could react, Paul lunged

toward his car. Ana yelled, "Hey!" and Maiv shouted "Wait!" but he slammed and locked the door behind him and peeled out of the parking lot without a backward glance.

Colin swore loudly. "Way to leave us stranded, man!" he shouted after the car.

"Now what?" said James. The headlights were getting steadily closer.

Maiv braced herself. "Run."

CHAPTER 3
COLIN

The four of them sprinted back toward the van.

Colin heard squealing tires and saw the headlights beaming from behind, lighting up the road ahead of him. Paul had gotten away clean and left them to fend for themselves. And now the Benefactor, or the Benefactor's goon, was closing in on them.

"Where do we go?" he shouted to Maiv.

"Back south toward downtown," Maiv gasped back.

James was up ahead, practically dragging Ana along beside him. *"Get in get in get in!"* he shouted over his shoulder to Colin and Maiv.

Two seconds later Colin was in the driver's seat, veering onto the road. A car was right behind them. Colin half-expected it to ram straight into the back of the van.

But he floored the gas and managed to stay just ahead of the other vehicle.

Colin had no idea how to lose a tail. Plus the van probably had a tracker. So it was going to take some fancy moves to get everyone out of this.

Downtown. Where the streets were complicated and lots of cops hung out. The driver behind them wouldn't try to shoot them there. And maybe they could lose him.

At the last second, Colin took a sharp right onto a side street. The van started to tip to one side but then righted itself. Colin slammed on the gas. He could see Maiv out of the corner of his eye, holding tightly to her seat and the door handle.

Headlights flashed in his rearview mirror and he knew the car had made the turn. Colin flew down the road and took another right onto a one-way street. Before the other car could make it, Colin veered into an alley and sped through to the other side—another one-way street going in the opposite direction.

He did this five more times: tight turn, turn into alley, cross back until he was almost where he started.

The car that had been following them was nowhere in sight.

Maiv pointed to a parking garage and Colin squealed in, going all the way up to the top of the ramp. Once he'd parked, no one moved for a minute. Colin tried to control his breathing. He was suddenly so tired, he wasn't sure he could get out of the van. But the Benefactor would be catching up to them soon. They needed to get away from this van and find someplace safe.

Colin opened the door and the other three followed suit. This time Colin noticed that Maiv brought a backpack and Ana carried a duffel bag.

"We have to ditch the van," said Maiv. "Oh, and our phones. Anything the Benefactor could be tracking."

"I have a tablet the Benefactor doesn't know about," said Ana.

Maiv nodded. "Great, keep it. I've got a burner phone. But anything that's traceable has to stay here."

"Not *here* here," Ana protested. "Then if the police find the van, they'll connect it with us right away."

"They'll connect it to me pretty fast anyway," Colin pointed out, shrugging. "I had to rent it under my name." He took his cell phone out of his jeans pocket. With a pang, he thought of his mom and sister texting him, calling him, trying to make sure he was OK.

James was clearly thinking along the same lines. "What about my family?" he asked, sounding panicked. "They think I ran away. My grandpa's dying, and my aunt doesn't have anybody else. I have to let them know I'm OK."

"We'll get burner phones for you and Colin once we're clear of here," Maiv told him. "If you need to contact anybody, you can do it then. But we'll still have to be really careful, because our families' phones may be bugged too."

Colin nodded. He couldn't help being impressed by Maiv's quick thinking under pressure. Radio silence would be tough, but it just might keep their loved ones safe from the Benefactor.

Ana held the empty gun between her forefinger and her thumb. "I don't know about the rest of you, but I've had enough of guns to last the rest of my life."

"Hallelujah," said James, and the others agreed.

"Agreed," said Maiv. "Let's get rid of that too."

Colin helped Ana take the gun apart. On the way out of the parking garage, they tossed the gun's parts and their phones into four different garbage cans.

Outside, Colin said, "My sister and I went to this all-night diner once. It's a few streets over. The only people that go there are regulars and drunk people. We should be able to talk there."

James shrugged and Ana nodded. Maiv said, "Lead the way." So Colin led them down two scary alleys and through one parking lot, keeping his eye out for any strange cars moving slowly. So far so good. If they could just catch their breath . . .

There it was. Colin could smell the frying oil from where he stood.

Inside, the four of them slid into a booth. There were blinds over the window, Colin noted with approval. He had a good view of the front door. And behind him were the bathrooms and the back exit. They had a way out if they needed one.

A server slopped some water in front of them along with some menus. He didn't even say hi. Colin couldn't have cared less. After the server left, the four of them didn't say a word for a full minute. Ana was shivering. James took off his jacket and gave it to her. She managed a shaky smile in return.

Maiv let out a big breath. "OK. So let's take stock of what we've got. My burner phone and Ana's tablet, the file from SolarStar—"

"And zero help from Paul," said Colin bitterly. He was still furious that an adult—with a gun that was probably actually loaded—had abandoned four teens without a second thought.

His dad never would've done something like that, or his mom. But then, he'd been lucky to have parents who didn't just look out for themselves. He wanted to be that kind of person too. Colin silently vowed that he would stick with this group—that he would have their backs. He didn't know them, not really. But he wouldn't leave them behind as long as any of them were in danger.

James opened the folder. "I'm guessing the file's going to be the most help? If we can figure out what it is."

"I'm pretty sure those are schematics. Let me take a look," Maiv said, holding out her hand. James handed it over and Maiv studied the pages inside. "Yeah, they're definitely schematics for something—I'd guess a vehicle."

"I have some files from EarthWatch," Ana added. "They were on a flash drive that I stole and was supposed to destroy. But I copied the files before I ruined the drive. They're on my tablet now."

Maiv nodded, looking relieved. "Excellent. That means nothing we tampered with is lost for good. We have to return this stuff as soon as possible."

"Without getting arrested for stealing it," added James.

Ana shifted in her seat and said, "I need to get my sister, you guys. Like, now. Izzy's only eight. And I have to get her tonight, while she's staying at her friend's house. Before she goes back to the Davenports—our foster parents. They'll try to get her to tell them where I am. She doesn't know, but if she won't say anything they might—hurt her."

Colin knew how it felt to worry about a sibling's safety. "OK, two priorities: we need to find a safe place, and we need to get Izzy."

"Which means a motel," said Maiv.

"Are any of us old enough to rent a motel room?" asked James.

Colin grinned. "According to the fake ID the Benefactor gave me, I am."

"Yeah, there's no way he can track an ID, just a credit card. So we just need enough money to pay for a room," said Maiv.

"Um," said James, "isn't that what got us all

into this mess in the first place? The fact that none of us have money?"

Ana reached into her backpack. "I have a little cash saved up. It's not much, but it'll cover the cost of a room for a few nights, plus some food. And a cab to get there."

Maiv reached into her backpack. "I'll call a cab on my burner phone. And once we're settled, we'll make a plan."

CHAPTER 4

ANA

Inside the motel room, they collapsed—Maiv
and Ana on the bed, James on the only chair,
and Colin on the floor.

It was almost 2:30 am. It had been just an
hour since Ana's whole life had changed.

Ana immediately pulled out her tablet and
started tapping away.

"Writing to Izzy?" Maiv asked. Ana nodded.

More quietly, Maiv said, "The Benefactor
could be tracking her phone."

Ana kept typing, trying to find the right
words. "I know. But I'm texting her in code.

The Benefactor doesn't know about the code. We were in a public park when we thought it up—no bugs, no spies listening in."

Maiv muttered what sounded like, "Ima Contestant."

Ana smiled briefly. "Yep. And now I'm going to get a cab and go pick her up."

Colin spoke up. "Do you think that's safe?"

Grimly, Ana said, "Safer than leaving her at the mercy of the Benefactor. Or our foster dad."

"Ana, if the Benefactor knows where Izzy is, you can't risk going there," Maiv said, tucking the hair behind her ears.

For the first time, Ana stopped texting and looked up. She shot a fierce look at Maiv. "I am *not* leaving her alone."

Maiv put her hands up. "I get it. I do. I have siblings too."

Ana seriously doubted that she "got it." She said, "Izzy's all I have. And I'm all she has. Nothing in this world matters more to me, do you understand? If you're too worried, I'll leave now and do my own thing."

James stepped in. "You don't need to do

that. I think sticking together is the way to get through this." He looked from Ana to Maiv. "Let's find a way to get Izzy here."

Maiv sighed and nodded. "OK, we can figure this out. None of us can go pick her up—that's too dangerous. Someone could be tracking her movements, watching the place where she's staying." Then Maiv sat up straighter. "But—maybe we can send someone else."

Ana's eyes narrowed. "Like who?"

***

It took close to ten minutes for Maiv to convince Ana, but finally Ana gave in. She sat beside Maiv as Maiv held her phone in front of them and spoke to her friend Adam on speaker.

"Adam, I'm sorry to wake you up."

"Maiv, is that you? I don't know this number."

"Yeah, it's me. Long story. So, uh, do you remember you said you would do me a favor if I needed one?"

The guy sounded more awake now. "Of

course. Holy—Maiv, it's almost three in the morning. Where've you been? Are you home now? Your parents called—"

"I'll explain soon. But don't call my parents or tell anyone you've heard from me. Right now I need you to get a cab, go to the address I give you, and wait for an eight-year-old girl to come out of the house and get into the cab with you. And then—"

"What in the name of—"

"*And then*," Maiv steamrolled over him, "I need you to have the cab take you both to the motel address I'm about to give you and meet us here."

"Us?"

"I told you it's a long story. Do you have something to write the addresses down with?"

"Maiv, this sounds insane. Are you asking me to kidnap someone?"

"No," Ana cut in. "She's asking you to save someone from being kidnapped. We're talking about my sister, and she's in danger. Maiv said we could trust you. Are you going to help or not?"

There was the briefest pause before Adam

said, "Of course I'll help. In any way I can. Hit me with those addresses, Maiv."

Maiv breathed out, and Ana relaxed just the tiniest bit. Maiv said into the phone, "Thank you, Adam." She grinned at Ana and mouthed, "He's really great." Ana smiled back.

She immediately texted Izzy again, still using the code they'd invented together. It was weird to tell Izzy to get in a cab with a stranger, but she knew Izzy trusted her.

"Will she be able to get out of the friend's house without anyone noticing?" Colin asked.

"Oh yeah," said Ana. "She's my sister. She knows how to get out when she needs to."

***

With nothing to do but wait, Colin said, "There's got to be a late-night convenience store within walking distance. I can go pick up something to eat. Why didn't we order anything at the diner?"

James snorted. "Yeah, then maybe we wouldn't have gotten that death stare from the server."

Amused in spite of herself, Ana said, "We left him a tip, though. He can't be that mad."

Colin got up and stretched.

"I'll go with you," Maiv said. "Safety in numbers. Um—Ana, could we borrow some more of your cash?"

"Sure." Ana took out a $20 bill just as her phone buzzed. Izzy had texted back with their code word for "OK." And then *corazón*—their code word for "love."

Ana breathed out. Soon they'd be back together—though not exactly safe.

Next she texted her friend Emma: *Open the email.*

Emma would know what that meant. Ana had evidence of her foster dad's abuse. She'd emailed that evidence to Emma, with the subject line DO NOT OPEN UNLESS I TEXT YOU. She knew Emma would share what she saw with her mother—an attorney— and phone calls would be made. Her foster parents were not going to get their hands on Izzy again. Ana could make sure of that much, at least.

Fifteen minutes later Maiv and Colin were back with cheap sandwiches for everyone.

"This is seriously the best sandwich I've ever had," said James as he dug into his.

Ana couldn't eat yet. Not until Izzy was with her, safe and sound. She watched her tablet, waiting for another text.

But she noticed when Maiv pulled a tiny notebook and a pen out of her backpack.

"OK, let's go over what we know," Maiv said.

"Uh . . ." said James. "I know basically nothing right now."

"OK, well, we'll start at the beginning."

"Aren't you going to tell us who the Benefactor is?" said Ana. "Because the suspense is starting to get to me."

"Let's put all the pieces together first," said Maiv. "Then I'll tell you my theory, and you can let me know whether you agree with me, based on all the facts."

"That's fair," said Colin.

Ana sighed and went back to staring at her

tablet, but she couldn't help listening.

"To start with, we know that the Benefactor's goal was to steal—and probably destroy—this file from SolarStar. The file contains schematics for some kind of new product that's supposed to be a team effort between SolarStar and EarthWatch."

"EarthWatch is the company Paul Grayson used to work for?" James asked, and Maiv nodded.

"Right. It's an environmental think tank. SolarStar is an engineering firm that does lots of work with renewable energy— environmentally friendly technologies. So EarthWatch came up with this idea, and SolarStar is going to produce it, whatever 'it' is. Everyone with me so far?"

"Sorrrrrt of," said James. "Keep going, I'll get there."

Maiv took his word for it. "OK, now, Alfred Huffmann Industries is partnering with SolarStar, giving them the money they need to actually make this project a reality . . ."

Ana looked up sharply. "Huffmann Industries?"

"Ring a bell?" asked Colin.

"My foster dad has worked with them. He's a big-shot lawyer. And a terrible person," she couldn't resist adding, just for the record.

Colin sat up straight. "Could he be the Benefactor?"

"The Benefactor is definitely someone tied to Huffmann Industries, but I don't think it's Ana's foster dad," said Maiv.

"Yeah, Huffmann Industries is the link, for sure," Colin agreed. "They were on the verge of making a big deal with an oil company, but then they backed out and changed directions entirely. They teamed up with SolarStar instead. So over here you've got oil." He lifted his right hand, which still held his half-eaten sandwich, angling it to the right. "And way over here you've got, like, water power and wind power and solar power and stuff like that." He held up his other hand and stretched it as far to the left as possible. "And the people who like oil don't tend to like green energy, and vice versa."

"In other words," continued Maiv, "someone wanted Huffmann Industries to partner with an oil company and got very, very angry when it partnered with SolarStar instead."

"And that's the Benefactor," said James.

"I think so. I think this whole Contest was designed to get us to ruin the SolarStar project with Huffmann Industries."

"You seriously think someone went to all this trouble just for that?" said Ana skeptically, nodding at the file folder.

Maiv nodded. "Think about it. If this project falls apart, that's a major embarrassment and annoyance for Huffmann Industries. And it definitely looks as if it's SolarStar's and EarthWatch's fault for not protecting their information. So then, maybe, Huffmann Industries decides not to work with them anymore and goes back to partnering with more reliable businesses, like oil companies. And the Benefactor wins."

"So who *is* the Benefactor?" Ana said,

throwing up her hands. "In your opinion, anyway."

Maiv took a deep breath. "Alfred Huffmann, the retired founder of Huffmann Industries."

CHAPTER 5

COLIN

Colin glanced at James and Ana: blank looks from both of them. "OK . . . so if he's retired, why does he care what the company does now?"

Maiv started pacing back and forth. "Lots of reasons, I imagine. Pride, partly. His daughter is the CEO now, and from what I've gathered, they have very different ideas about how to run the company. And of course, he still owns lots of shares in the company, so when Huffmann Industries does well, he makes money. And even shadier: I found out that he owns a whole bunch of shares in ChemOil, the oil company that Huffmann Industries almost teamed up with. So if that deal had actually happened, he would have made billions on top of billions."

A lightbulb went off for Colin. "I'll bet he was the anonymous source in an article I read—totally bashing the SolarStar deal."

"So let me see if I've got this straight," said James. "Huffmann is pissed that the oil company deal fell apart. His daughter's taking the company in a completely different direction. Plus he doesn't make any money for himself."

Maiv nodded. "Right. Which is why he wants to destroy the project. And I'm guessing he hopes this will make his daughter change her mind about green energy. Once this project falls through, maybe Huffmann Industries will go back to the kind of projects he likes. The kind of projects that *he* can make money from."

Ana had to admit that this was starting to look like a possibility. "And he didn't want anything to get traced back to him. So he used us to take the fall for him."

Colin grunted in frustration. "But why us?"

There was a pause as all four of them tried to think. Colin put his head in his hands and scrubbed at his hair. He needed a shower . . .

Ana cleared her throat. "My foster dad works for Huffmann Industries, like I said. I don't know if he knew about any of this, but that at least explains how I'd be on Huffmann's radar."

James said, "There's no way they would know about me. I only have my aunt and my grandpa. And my aunt's been out of the country for a couple of years!"

Maiv looked at him sharply. "Doing what?"

"She worked for this charity called Doctors Together." Pride showed in his voice.

Maiv let out a breath. "Well, there you have it. In my research, I found that Doctors Together is a charity arm of Huffmann Industries. He must have done some digging to find you through your aunt."

James shook his head in disbelief. "This

dude . . . he's got some issues. So how are *you* connected?"

Maiv stopped pacing and sat down again. "When I figured out who the Benefactor was, I racked my brains for why he would know about me. And then I remembered that my dad does janitorial work in a bunch of office buildings, so I called the headquarters of Huffmann Industries and asked who the cleaning company is. Sure enough . . ."

Colin pulled his legs up to his chest. "This is nuts. I don't think I *ever* had any contact with them."

But then something came to mind. His dad had sometimes done handyman jobs to make a little extra money. "Actually, wait . . . my dad used to do odd jobs for rich people. I bet Huffmann hired him at some point. It had to have been years ago . . ." He let out a long breath. "Wow. My dad must have made an impression." He didn't doubt it. His dad had had the biggest personality of anyone he'd ever met.

Maiv tapped her pen against her notepad. "I think he's been masterminding this for a while. And I'm sure he had help. People bugging our homes, our phones, our devices. People watching us. And even people looking into our lives so that Huffmann would know how to push our buttons."

"That all makes sense," said Colin. "I mean, kind of, anyway. Like evil-genius-with-too-much-time-on-his-hands sense. But are we totally sure that this file was the endgame? That Huffmann doesn't have any other plans in motion?"

"Good point," said Maiv. "We need to be sure we have the full picture."

"It might be smart to go over all our tasks," Colin added.

James sat back and groaned.

Just then, Izzy texted Ana again. Ana let out a huge breath of relief. "She's in the cab!" she blurted out. "With Adam! She says she's OK! They'll be here soon."

It seemed as if the whole room was suddenly breathing more easily. Colin felt relieved and grateful for Ana's sake. Even though he wished his own sister was here, and his mom too.

"See?" James said gently to Ana. "It's going to be OK."

She smiled faintly. "I almost believe you."

CHAPTER 6

MAIV

Izzy came in shyly, but Ana seemed instantly stronger. She hugged Izzy hard before turning to Adam and Maiv. "Thank you," she said. "This means the world to me."

Izzy took one look around and said, "Can we order room service?"

Everyone cracked up. "Not now, kitten. You have to go back to sleep." Despite Izzy's protests, Ana bundled her into the motel bed, turning off the lamp on the side table. Meanwhile Maiv took Adam aside.

"I can't thank you enough."

"Hey, it worked out. I didn't get arrested or anything." He was joking, but the smile died as soon as he saw the look on Maiv's face. "Maiv, you have to tell me what's going on. Your parents are super worried. Nobody's seen you since you were at my house yesterday afternoon. You haven't been answering calls or texts . . ."

"I can't get into it right now, Adam. Just go home, and if you can talk to my parents outside or get them to come to your house, tell them that I'm safe, for now. And that I'm working something out. And that I'm so sorry. But I'm serious, you can't call them or text them or talk to them at our home."

"Safe *for now*? What are you mixed up in, Maiv? Who are these other people? What—"

"Later," said Maiv. "I swear. I'm only keeping you in the dark right now to protect you. The less you know, the safer you'll be. But at some point—I will tell you everything. I promise."

* * *

"All right," whispered Maiv after Adam had left. The four of them sat in the dark. She kept her voice low to avoid waking Izzy. "Let's go through all our tasks."

Ana bit her lip. "Listen, I'm not proud of the things I did. So I just want to say I'm sorry for whatever—"

James cut her off. "We all are, Ana. We made some bad choices. But for really good reasons, I bet. To help our families. And this guy took advantage of us. So let's just figure out how to make it right."

Ana nodded. Colin leaned forward and put his head in his hands and then sat back up. "OK, I'll go first."

After about fifteen minutes the four of them had laid out their tasks. Maiv wrote them down by the light of her phone, then organized them all into a time line for the past week and a half. She read it out loud.

Last week: Maiv wrote a story for her school newspaper about teen runaways. This would make Maiv's later disappearance seem like something she planned herself. Colin took video footage of Ana and Izzy at a park and sent a snap cutter to Ana's house. Maiv created a computer virus, put it on a jump drive, and sent it to Ana. Late Sunday night, Ana stood outside James's apartment with a banner that said 'We're waiting.'

Monday: Colin went to SolarStar to get footage of the office layout and to plant a bug in the office of Len Steinberg. He failed to plant the bug and then left it at Ana's house. Ana left the jump drive with Maiv's virus at James's apartment.

Tuesday: James left a note for the principal of Cleveland High School, saying that Maiv was cheating. Ana planted the bug in Steinberg's office. Maiv bought clothes and a burner phone to send to James.

Wednesday: James stole Ana's backpack. Maiv left a threatening note for Colin. Ana received Colin's footage of herself and Izzy—another threat. She used the snap cutter to damage the plumbing of Maiv's house. James spray-painted the outside wall of Colin's high school with a threat to Colin's family. Colin stole James's bike.

Thursday: Maiv delivered Colin's fake ID and credit card. Colin used these to buy a gun. Maiv put a threatening note in James's locker. James took the printed copy of Colin's family's insurance from their hardware store.

Friday: Maiv delivered fireworks to Ana's house. James released Maiv's virus at EarthWatch, probably wiping important info from their servers. Ana stole and destroyed a jump drive from EarthWatch, probably for the same reason. James also left a threatening voicemail for Paul, using the phone Maiv sent him.

Saturday: Ana took photos of Paul and his family and left them at James's apartment. James followed Paul, wearing the clothes Maiv sent him. He also delivered the photos to Paul's house. Colin delivered the gun to Ana's house. At midnight, Ana set off the fireworks behind Colin's family's store, setting it on fire.

Sunday: James left a package in a locker at the Amtrak station. Colin rented the van and drove it downtown. Ana planted the gun under a bench for James. Colin reverse-pickpocketed James to give him his instructions. James stole the file from Jennifer McKnight's office at StolarStar.

"Holy crap, this is insane," said Colin.

"Yeah," said James. "He didn't have ten tasks planned out ahead of time for each of us. He left himself a bunch of leeway, so he could make up stuff as he went along—tasks that would punish someone else, or fix someone else's mistakes."

"Or just get our fingerprints on things," added Maiv. "Or catch us on some security camera somewhere. So that we'd all take the fall, and no one would ever figure out that he was pulling the strings."

Maiv fought against the despair that gnawed at her. The Benefactor was a careful planner *and* good at thinking on his feet. He adjusted his plan every time the contestants tried to go off-script. How could they ever outwit this person? Especially since the Benefactor clearly had a lot of money and probably a lot of power. It was hopeless.

"But it looks like you were right, Maiv," said Ana. "Aside from the tasks that are just designed to scare us and keep us in line, everything's connected to ruining this one project. Erasing the records at EarthWatch and then stealing the hard copy."

"Except one thing," said James. "My eighth task doesn't line up with anything. That package I left at the Amtrak station—what do you think that was?"

Looking at the three of them—so keyed up, so ready to do whatever needed doing—Maiv felt the despair fade a little. They were in this together. "I don't know," she said. "But we can find out."

CHAPTER 7

COLIN

Colin pointed out that nobody could get to the St. Paul Amtrak station at four in the morning without a car, so they all agreed to get some sleep and deal with the next steps in a few hours.

But first, Colin had a plan to set in motion.

"Hey, Ana, can I borrow your tablet for a minute?"

She handed it over, and he prayed he was remembering his sister's phone number correctly. They'd gotten their first cell phones at the same time, in middle school, and for a while they'd been the only contacts in each other's phones. Those digits had been precious back then.

"What are you doing?" asked Maiv—always alert and keeping tabs on everything, Colin had noticed.

"Just texting my sister. In code, don't worry."

Maiv threw up her hands and laughed. "Does everyone have a code they use with their families?"

Colin smiled at her. "I'm making this one up as I go along. But I think Danni will get it."

The text said simply: *Question from a frequent customer. Do you sell used cars? I'll be stopping by tomorrow morning first thing to find out.*

***

Colin figured that the Benefactor wasn't monitoring Burnett Hardware anymore, now that it was mostly charred wood. At least that's what he hoped as he got off the bus and made his way to the parking lot behind the building at 7:30 in the morning.

Looking at the damage from the fire, he felt overwhelming sadness. His father had started this store. His optimistic, fun father who died way too young. And then he and his mom and Danni worked hard to keep it afloat.

All gone in one night. Because of him. One of the Benefactor's punishments would cost the Burnetts their business. And Colin had no idea how Danni would afford surgery now. Colin had ruined that chance for her. He was responsible for all this.

How could he ever tell his mom? Or Danni?

An ancient Toyota pulled into the parking lot. Colin didn't recognize the car. He stiffened.

But then his sister, Danni, got out. "Colin, what the ever-loving—"

Colin threw his arms around her. She hugged him back fiercely. "I *knew* that note was bull. I knew it. You don't walk out on things. What is going on? Mom's worried sick, like she wasn't already."

Colin stepped back. "Listen, Danni, I can't

stay long, but I need your help. And I can't tell you a lot about it. I need you to trust me."

Danni shook her head. "No way, little brother. Not this time. You need to talk to me. You are in trouble, and I am your family."

Colin felt tears in his eyes. "Tell Mom I'm all right. And tell her I'm sorry. And Danni . . . I'm sorry to you too. This is all my fault. I'm working to fix it, but you have to believe me when I say that you're in danger if I tell you more."

Danni crossed her arms. "Colin, I will follow you. I will pin you down. I will not let you go."

He knew Danni wasn't bluffing. "OK, here's what you can do. If you buy a burner phone, you can text me at the number I used before. I'm using a friend's phone for now, so I might not get back to you right away, but I'll do what I can to keep you posted."

Colin put his hands on Danni's shoulders. "But listen to me, Danni. You can't tell anyone you've seen me, understand?"

"I can't keep Mom in the dark!"

"Then make sure you take her somewhere outside or to a public place you wouldn't normally go to. The people I'm mixed up with, they've got bugs everywhere. And if they find me, they'll kill me. They might kill you too."

The blood drained out of Danni's face. "You realize you sound like you've gone off the deep end?"

"Yeah. But you trust me, right?"

Something in Colin's eyes must have talked her out of arguing. "Of course I trust you."

She held up the car key in her hand. "Why do you think I brought this piece of crap with me?"

***

They had wheels again. Colin felt safer already.

Danni had hit up a friend for a favor, and the guy had loaned Danni his car. It must have been a big favor, because Colin didn't think he'd ever lend a car to anyone, even if it wasn't the nicest car in the world.

This was a 1999 Corolla with rusted everything. The doors creaked. The floors were in bad shape. But it ran. And that was all Colin needed.

Operation Take Down the Benefactor was up and running.

CHAPTER 8

JAMES

"I don't like this," James said for the thousandth time.

Ana gave him the stink eye again. "It'll be fine. Now that you've given me the locker number and combo, it'll be a breeze." She was determined, he could tell.

But James had been antsy all morning. While Colin was getting transportation lined up, James and Maiv had done some shopping of their own. Using cash Ana had brought, they'd bought burner phones for James and Colin, plus breakfast. It had felt good to be outside again, to be doing something proactive. James felt as though he was the weak link in this group. He hadn't dug up any information about the Benefactor or even tried that hard to get out of the Contest. He felt like a fool now for believing the Benefactor had really planned to help. There had to be a way to make up for being so naive. There had to be a way for James to contribute.

Yet more than ever, he felt as if his hands were tied. Maiv said it wasn't safe for him to call or text his aunt, even with the new burner phone. The Benefactor might be monitoring Aunt Beth's phone too. "Then what's the point of having the burner phone?" James had asked her on the way back to the motel.

"So the four of us can communicate when and if we're separated," Maiv had said. A reasonable answer.

Except that James still didn't seem to be going anywhere. Ana and Colin were about to try to get the package at the Amtrak station. In fact, right now Colin was using Ana's tablet to look up the fastest way to get there. But James and Maiv were staying behind.

Izzy said, "I don't like it either." She sounded so serious that both Ana and James smiled.

James said, "Let's put on fake mustaches and we'll all go. But Izzy will do the talking."

Izzy giggled and playfully hit James on the shoulder. James pretended to collapse. "I mean look at that right hook!"

And smiled but then said, "No, I'm going. We have to get our hands on whatever's in that locker. And I don't live anywhere near the Amtrak station—unlike you and Maiv. And Colin is the getaway driver. So I'm the best person to actually go in."

Just then, Colin said, "Uh, you guys? You might want to take a look at this."

They all gathered around Ana's tablet. Colin had pulled up a local news site and was watching a clip from a report. He unplugged the earbuds so that they could all hear the video.

The outside of SolarStar's building flashed on the screen. A reporter said, "Security guards say an African American male and a Latina female were involved in the break-in. Downtown cameras show a white van with the license plate NHW736 idling down the block. The van appeared to have two other occupants—an Asian female and a white male. Police say this group is armed and dangerous. If you encounter them, proceed with caution. So far, no businesses in the building have reported anything stolen. Police believe this may be gang related. Brian, back to you."

James sat down hard.

They were fugitives. And of course: *gang related*. He didn't know whether to laugh or cry.

"Well, what should we call our gang?" he said sarcastically.

Colin snorted. "You got the spray painting part down, man. Just not the guns and drugs."

But Ana didn't look amused. She said quietly, "This was exactly what Huffmann was banking on, isn't it? People assuming things about us, writing us off, so that he could get away with his plan."

James didn't say anything. She was right, after all. People had been stereotyping him his whole life. The police wouldn't have trouble believing he was a criminal. Same with the other three, in one way or another, at least to some extent. Except for maybe Colin. But Colin's family was struggling, and someone who only knew what neighborhood he lived in might easily label him too. People looked at them, saw easy explanations, and didn't look any further. And the Benefactor had been counting on that.

Izzy reached out to take Ana's hand. Sweet Izzy, who wouldn't get a fair shake either. James saw the love in Ana's eyes when she looked at her sister. She stood up again.

"Colin and I are going to the Amtrak station to see if that package is still where James left it. Meanwhile"—she looked at Maiv and James— "you two figure out how we can hold Huffmann accountable for this."

CHAPTER 3

ANA

Ana's insides were shaking as Colin's car pulled up in front of the Amtrak station. She took a deep breath. "So you'll wait in the parking lot?"

"Yeah, it'll look weird if I sit here idling," said Colin. "But I'll be ready for a quick getaway."

"We probably won't need it. Huffmann can't be monitoring all the places we've gone."

"But the cops might have ID'd us from the SolarStar break-in. Our pictures could be circulating by now."

"So my goals are to grab the box and stay under the radar."

"Right," said Colin. "You got this."

Ana smiled at him and got out of the car. She hoped she looked confident as she walked into the station.

Inside, she took a quick look up and saw two security cameras facing the ticket desk.

A lady at the ticket counter saw her and narrowed her eyes. Ana threw her a big smile and headed toward the lockers.

She hurried down the row of lockers, looking for the right number. She turned the corner—and there, sitting at a little table, drinking coffee, were two police officers.

Ana practically skidded to a halt and then cursed herself. If they noticed that, it was a dead giveaway she was up to something shady.

Of course, the locker she needed was halfway down the row. Almost directly across from the officers.

My luck. But she needed to find out what was in that locker. She just hoped that Huffmann or someone else hadn't already collected it.

Ana stood in front of the locker, her back to

the cops, and put in the combination that James had given her.

Nothing happened.

She tried again. Nothing.

Sweat started down her temple. Could he have given her the wrong numbers? She took a deep breath and tried it one more time. Success! She had been shaking too badly to do it right the first couple of times.

She yanked the door open and saw it: a cardboard box. No one had taken it yet. She grabbed it, closed the door quietly, and spun around.

Right into a guy who had been standing right behind her.

"Yer pretty," the guy said. Ana could smell the alcohol oozing out of him. He smelled like her foster dad. The guy had bloodshot eyes and few teeth. He said, "Could a pretty lady give me a dollar?" He held out his hand. Ana felt for the man. But she did not have time for this.

"Sorry," she mumbled and stepped around him. But he stepped right back in front of her.

"Pretty ladies should be nicer," he said, his voice rising.

Ana glanced nervously at the cops. So far, they weren't paying attention. "Uh, true. Good luck!"

She stepped around him again but this time he grabbed her arm. "What's one dollar to a pretty lady like you?"

And suddenly, the two cops were right there. Ana knew she looked panicked, but she hoped they wouldn't think it was because of them.

"Is this man bothering you?" one of the officers asked.

"Um, I'm just leaving. It's no big deal."

The other cop was looking at her intently. "Have I seen you somewhere?"

She shook her head. "I don't think so, officer." Her voice squeaked at the end. She kept walking, forcing herself not to run.

The homeless guy said, "I was just asking this pretty lady if she wanted to get rid of a dollar."

The first cop nodded and said, "Well, you can't bother people about it, OK? Maybe we can get you some coffee or . . . ?"

Ana was almost to the end of the hallway when the other cop said to his partner, "I just got why she looks familiar." When she turned the corner, she didn't look back. She ran.

Luckily, a train had just pulled up and people were getting out. Ana weaved in and out of the crowd. Behind her she heard the officer yell, "Hey!" and then a few seconds later, "Did you see a Latina girl, maybe five-three . . . ?"

Ana reached the door and booked it across the parking lot toward Colin's rickety car. She jumped into the passenger seat, then ducked way down, sliding into the footwell.

"Drive normally," she whispered, "and don't look down." Colin nodded just barely, and she felt the car start moving.

A minute or so later, Colin said, "We're clear."

Ana sat up, clutching the package to her chest, and grabbed her seatbelt. "Well," she said, "our pictures are definitely circulating."

CHAPTER 10

COLIN

When Colin and Ana got back to the motel
room, Izzy jumped into Ana's arms. "James
showed me how to draw unicorns! But not dumb
unicorns—unicorns that can stab people with
their horns."

Ana looked at James, and he gave her a small
wink. "Um, good, I guess?" she said with a laugh.

"Yep," he said. "Your sister is pretty much
a genius."

Ana smoothed out Izzy's hair. "Well, I
could've told you that." She set the package on
the bed.

"You got it!" said James.

"Just barely. Ready to open it?"

All four of them sat around the bed, like they were about to do some weird ritual. No one touched the box. Finally, Colin couldn't stand it anymore. "I'll do it!" he said.

He ripped it open and found—a mostly empty box. Except for another file folder. Always file folders.

A single sheet of paper was inside the folder. He had to read it twice to let it sink in. Then he read it aloud to the others.

To Whom It May Concern:

We, the undersigned, hereby confess to robbing SolarStar and sabotaging EarthWatch. We worked together under the direction of Paul Grayson. We take this opportunity to claim the credit for our cleverness. You can try to find us, but you will not succeed. It has been very easy to dupe you so far. Good luck in your investigation.

Signed:

Maiv Moua

Colin Burnett

James Trudeleau

Ana Rivera

He flipped the paper around so they could all see it. "I don't know about the rest of you," he said, "but that signature looks a lot like my actual handwriting."

"Yeah," said Maiv. "Add 'forgery' to the list of Huffmann's skills."

"Or skills he can hire other people for," added Ana. "This would've looked pretty convincing if the cops had found it."

"Luckily, we got hold of it first." Colin tore the paper into tiny pieces. It felt good. "Well, that takes care of that."

But he could tell Maiv was still upset. She covered her face with her hands. "I can't believe I let this happen. I entered this stupid thing, and I *knew*. I just knew it was a bad idea. It's like responding to a chain letter! Who *does* that?"

"Hey," said Ana, "None of us are stupid, and we all fell for it. I had my suspicions too. But the Benefactor knew such specific things about us. It didn't seem like a run-of-the-mill scam. And I guess it wasn't. Plus, I don't think he would've taken no for an answer. He was prepared to force us to do what he wanted, right from the beginning."

Maiv let her hands drop. She sighed and looked up at the ceiling. "He really did have me all figured out. I needed money for college. And both my mom and dad are in a lot of pain so they have a hard time working. I wanted to give them a break. I just didn't see another way out. How could I go to school and leave my parents with my five brothers and sisters? This contest seemed like a solution."

Ana patted Maiv's knee, her eyes shiny with tears. "I felt the same way. I didn't see how I could get Izzy out of the Davenports' place without putting us back in the foster system. I was willing to do anything to keep her safe and to keep us together. I was primed for this."

James sighed. "Well, count me in this club. My grandpa could have had this experimental treatment for his cancer if I'd gotten the money. But now it doesn't look like he'll . . ." James trailed off and looked away. When he looked back at all of them, his eyes were so sad Colin felt like a fist had punched him in the gut. Colin could never forget what losing his dad had felt like. James was going through that now. "At least I have my aunt Beth, though. Assuming I get out of this alive."

Colin wondered if he could tell them his own reasons for joining the Contest. It was clear they all cared about their families. Just like he cared about his. He cleared his throat. "My dad left us the hardware store when he died. We're in debt, and I knew we could lose the store soon. I wanted to help my mom out." He ran his hand through his hair. "And also, my sister, Danni—she's transgender. Biologically, she's male. I wanted to pay for her to have gender-reassignment surgery, which she really wants . . ."

James thumped his back in a "sorry, man" kind of way, and Maiv squeezed his arm. "You'll work it out," said Maiv softly. "Once we've sorted through all this. You'll figure something out."

"And hey, your insurance papers are still at my apartment," said James. "So you can get those back, at least."

"Yeah," said Colin, gratitude flowing through him. "Thanks, man."

"It's my fault your store burned down," added Ana. "I set off those fireworks. If there were anything I could do to help make up for it . . ."

They didn't even blink about Danni. In that moment, Colin loved every single one of them. He knew from experience the rest of the world wasn't always as accepting.

"You're making up for it now," he told Ana. "More than making up for it. All of you."

Izzy made a *yuck* face. "You guys are kind of mushy." Everyone laughed.

Colin wiped his eyes.

CHAPTER 11

ANA

"I'm going to grab some snacks for this little kitten," Ana said, smiling at Izzy. "Does anyone want anything?" All of them did, so James said he'd walk with her to the gas station.

On way there, James said, "I'm sorry about—all the stuff you're dealing with."

Ana sighed and said, "I'm sorry about your grandpa. It's got to be hard enough to deal with the fact that you're losing him, without all this on top of it."

"Yeah. But you know, my parents died

when I was pretty little. And I felt really bad about that for a long time. I still do. I went to live with my grandpa, and it's just in the last few years that I realized how lucky I was. He loves me so much. Just like my parents did. Knowing I've had that—it doesn't make losing it any easier. But I know it's always going to be there, that love of his. I wish everyone could have that."

James looked at her with such empathy . . . More than anything he said, his eyes showed how much he cared. Other than Izzy, Ana was pretty sure no one had cared about her in years.

And without warning, she was crying. Something in her broke wide open.

She thought James might freak out, but instead he put his arm around her. It felt so good that she cried right into his shoulder.

Ana was still amazed sometimes at how unfair the world was. Yet even after everything that had happened to James, he still used the word *lucky*. And she knew what he meant. She had Izzy. And now she had these three people watching her back.

She stood back and wiped her eyes. "I think you're a really good person."

"Thanks. I think you are too."

The moment had gotten super heavy, so Ana said, "We'd better hurry back, or else Izzy might start gnawing on Colin's leg or something."

James laughed. "Well, that wouldn't be good. We're already in enough trouble as it is."

"True." Something else had occurred to her. "There'll probably be security cameras in that convenience store. If anyone recognizes us, the cops will be sniffing around this neighborhood really soon. We can't keep hiding out here much longer. I feel like we're just sitting around, doing nothing."

James nodded. "Yeah, but Maiv will think of something. I trust her." He paused. "I trust all of you, actually." Then he laughed. "Though I also trusted some wacked-out contest that said it would give me $10 million."

Ana let out a shaky laugh. "We all did that. But now we're here, helping each other instead of working against each other. That's something, right?"

James smiled. "Yeah. That's something."

CHAPTER 12

MAIV

"I have an idea," Maiv announced when Ana and James got back from the store.

"And I," said James, "have coffee for everyone."

"You are a god among men," said Colin. "Let's have it."

Ana and James sat on the bed with Izzy, while Colin sat in the chair, and Maiv paced she talked.

Maiv wasn't at all sure her plan would work. But she did know it was risky. After she explained, the others sat back and just looked at her.

James cleared his throat. "So all of this has to go exactly right or we'll pretty much get caught and put in jail, and-or killed." He said it like a statement.

"Pretty much," Maiv confirmed.

Colin took a long slurp of his coffee. "Well, I'm in," he said. Maiv looked at him in surprise. She thought for sure she'd have a lot more convincing to do.

Ana laced her hands in front of her and leaned on her knees. "This plan has a lot of moving parts and a lot of ifs. But I think it's our only bet."

James took a deep breath. "Yeah. Let's do it."

Maiv could hardly believe it. They were all on board. She just hoped she wouldn't let them down.

* * *

"Talk us through it one more time," said James as Maiv swiped back and forth on Ana's tablet.

Maiv nodded as her fingers moved over the touchscreen. She didn't stop as she talked—too much to do. They needed this to end and now.

"First, I'm finding out Huffmann's phone number." And like magic as she said the words, there was his phone number.

She opened a different tab and began downloading some software. It would take awhile. She sat back on her heels and looked up at all of them. "Now I'm downloading spy software to put on his phone. And that's where you come in, James. If you're up for it."

James nodded, eyes wide but his face set in determination. "I'm up for it."

Maiv went on, "OK. So I've already downloaded a voice-modifying app that will disguise your voice when you call someone."

"I always wanted to sound like Darth Vader," said James.

"You're welcome," said Maiv with a small smile. "So you'll call him and deliver the message we agreed on." She chewed on her lip, her insides shaky at the thought. "And that's when I record his voice, admitting to what he's done."

Colin let out a huff of breath and leaned back. "And then how do we get the police to listen to us?"

The software was done downloading. Maiv typed Huffmann's phone number into the software and waited for that to register. "We don't go to the police. We go to SolarStar."

Ana said, "That's smart. Let *them* call the police. And if the SolarStar people don't believe us, we can bolt if we need to."

Maiv looked at James. He scooted closer to her so that he could easily talk into the tablet. "Ready?"

He nodded.

"Then I guess it's time to blackmail Alfred Huffmann."

CHAPTER 13
JAMES

"Remember, I'm putting it on speaker so everyone can hear the call," said Maiv. "So the rest of us have to be really quiet. First we'll do a test call to make sure the recording software works." She gave James the thumbs up.

The call went to Huffmann's voicemail. They'd expected that—no one answered a number they didn't know. James hung up and Maiv checked to make sure the software had done its job. Sure enough, Huffmann's voicemail message came out loud and clear when she played back the recording.

Colin said, "OK, James, work your magic."

James managed to grin at him. "Watch the master!" He cracked his knuckles and then hit the call icon again.

This time he waited for the beep and said, "Alfred Huffmann. I know you killed four people—Maiv Moua, James Trudeleau, Colin Burnett, and Ana Rivera. I have proof. Call this number back if you don't want to go to jail forever."

James hung up fast and then wiped his hands on his jeans. Colin patted him on the shoulder, and Ana silently applauded.

"Nice job," Maiv said. "And now we wait. We'll give him a day—" but the tablet immediately lit up with another call. James stiffened. He whispered, "It's him."

Maiv scrambled to start the recording again, then nodded to James.

Here we go. The real deal. James hit the green phone icon on the screen. "Huffmann?"

"Who is this?" Huffmann's gruff voice demanded. "How did you get this number?"

"I'll ask the questions, Mr. Huffmann. My

first is: how could you kill those four people?"

Huffmann snorted. "I have no idea what you're talking about."

"Sure," said James sarcastically. "Then I guess we have nothing else to say to each other."

"Hold on," said Huffmann sharply. "What four kids are you talking about?"

James almost punched the air in triumph. He could see that Maiv had caught it too. "I didn't say kids."

Huffmann hung up.

Maiv let out a long breath. "OK, so far so good. My guess is he'll be talking to his security person and trying to trace the call. He *will* call back. But this means we all have to be ready to move."

Ana asked, "Will he know he's being recorded?"

Maiv shook her head. "I coded and changed the software to be shielded. But he'll track the call, pinpoint Ana's tablet, and use its location to find us. That's why we have to stay one step ahead of him."

Ana moved closer to Izzy. "We're taking a

lot for granted here." James couldn't disagree.

The phone rang again, and James answered it, feeling a lot less shaky. The four of them had worked out this part of the conversation in advance. He had a script in his head for what he needed to say.

"I want to make a deal," he said.

Huffmann said, "I'm not saying anything. I'm calling back purely for entertainment. That said, I haven't heard about the deaths of any kids."

They had prepped for this. James said, "You're right. The kids aren't dead. But I know where they are."

There was silence on the other end of the line. James imagined Huffmann frantically signaling to whomever was in the room with him. Finally, Huffmann said, "I think finding lost children is always good. What can I do to help with this?"

James laughed. "I want $10 million. I want you to drop it off in the garbage can outside the SolarStar building at Nicollet Mall."

Again, silence on the other line. Finally, "$10

million is a ridiculous amount of money."

Real rage took over James. "Isn't that what you offered *them*? Ten million dollars in exchange for destroying SolarStar's new project?"

The silence on the other end seemed heavy this time. Ana was holding Izzy tightly, and Izzy had a hand over her mouth to show she was serious about keeping quiet. Colin clenched and unclenched his fists, and Maiv just bit her lip.

This could work or go completely south.

Huffmann said quietly, "You know, that $10 million prize is still out there. If you know the contestants, you should tell them that if one of them hands in that file, the money could be theirs."

James almost fainted with happiness. *He did it. He confessed to it.* But he kept his voice level.

"They're not interested, Mr. Huffmann."

Then Huffmann's voice got hard. "Well, then you may want to tell them that I'm still keeping tabs on their families. And if they don't want anyone to get hurt, they had better come in for their prize money."

James said, "Nicollet. Garbage. Today. Five

o'clock." And then he slammed his finger onto the screen to end the call.

Maiv stopped the recording and then replayed the whole exchange.

When it finished, something seemed to burst in all of them at the same time. "Yes!" shouted Colin, thumping James on the back. "Awesome job, man!"

They all started high-fiving. James and Ana missed, which made them both laugh hysterically, and then Ana leaned over and gave him a quick hug.

It was all there. They had their proof.

CHAPTER 14
ANA

Five minutes later, they all piled into the car. As Colin pulled out of the parking lot, Ana called SolarStar's main number. *Please pick up, please pick up.* Huffmann could be zeroing in on them already.

"SolarStar, this is Corey. How may I help you?"

Ana put on her businesslike voice. "I need to talk to Len Steinberg, immediately. Don't transfer my call—it's been dropped before. Bring him out to the front desk. Have him use your phone. This is extremely important."

"Uh . . . Oh . . . kay . . . Just a minute."

The others were watching her expectantly. She gave them a little grimace and a half-shrug. At least the receptionist hadn't hung up on her.

The sound of a phone fumbling gave way to a clear, familiar voice. "This is Len Steinberg."

Ana cleared her throat. "Mr. Steinberg, we have some material we think is crucial to you. It involves companies you're working with. Can you meet us at the front desk in a half an hour?"

Len Steinberg said, "What kind of information?"

Ana was prepared. "Information that could save your company."

But she wasn't prepared for the laugh that followed. "Well, I'm sorry but you'll have to be more specific. Especially since our company isn't in trouble."

Ana thought fast. "It has to do with the schematics you received from EarthWatch, which I believe are currently missing from Ms. McKnight's office. We'll see you in a half hour?"

The phone was silent for a full twenty seconds. Then: "All right."

Ana hung up, shaking. "Did it work?" asked Izzy.

Ana kissed the top of her sister's head. "So far."

Izzy was being so brave. She had been through so much already. And now she just might watch her big sister go to jail.

But at least neither of them would go back to the Davenports. Whatever happened next. Thanks to the evidence Ana had collected, the Davenports would get what they deserved. Now Ana just had to hope that the Benefactor would get what he deserved too.

As Colin exited the freeway, the buildings of downtown loomed above them. Just last night, they'd been speeding away from the SolarStar building, driving to what could have been their deaths. They were still in danger. In fact, they were driving right toward it, once again.

* * *

Colin found street parking, and they all got out, Izzy included. They walked in silence to the SolarStar building. James carried the SolarStar file. Ana clutched her tablet with numb hands.

She knew they'd only get one shot at this.

The moment they stepped into the lobby, a man and a woman in sharp suits turned toward them.

A badge flashed in the man's hand. "FBI, kids. Better come in."

CHAPTER 15

COLIN

Colin fought down panic. FBI.

"I'm Agent McElroy," said the guy, "and this is Agent Sydney. We need to speak with you." The agents ushered all five of them to the elevator.

"Sir and ma'am—" Colin started, but the guy shut him down with a stern look and pressed the button for the fifteenth floor. Colin's palms were slippery with sweat.

There was no turning back now.

* * *

Inside the SolarStar offices, the agents led the way to a conference room. Len Steinberg sat there with some other people Colin didn't recognize. Colin shot Steinberg a sheepish look. The only other time they'd met, Colin had been lying to Steinberg and trying to bug his office. He hadn't made a wildly successful first impression.

But Steinberg gave him a small smile, and Colin felt a little better. Maybe that meant these people would listen.

Agent McElroy motioned for all of them to sit down. Then he said, "Len Steinberg called us after you called him. We've been looking into this SolarStar sabotage since it started. Mr. Steinberg here has known for quite a while that something was going on."

Agent Sydney added, "But now we think you should tell us how you're involved."

James pulled out the schematics. "First, here are the plans I took. I didn't know what they were at the time. I'm sorry."

Ana spoke up quickly. "But James didn't do it alone. We were all part of this." She held up her tablet. "And I have information from your business partner, EarthWatch. I was supposed to destroy it, but I saved copies. I hope we haven't done any permanent damage to your project."

"This it wasn't our idea," Colin added. "We were all in the dark about the real purpose."

The room was silent. Steinberg grabbed the file folder and looked over the schematics. Then he nodded at the agents. Agent McElroy said, "OK. How about you start at the beginning?"

Maiv took a deep breath. "Right. Here's what happened."

When she finished, Len Steinberg took off his glasses and rubbed his nose. The agents looked at each other again. But Colin had hope. They weren't dismissing the story outright.

Maiv sat back in her chair, looking exhausted. "I'm guessing you won't find the website for the Contest or the emails the Benefactor sent us. But we do have evidence that Alfred Huffmann masterminded this. Ana, play the recording."

Ana took out her tablet and called up the soundbite. She played it for everyone in the room.

Even the FBI agents looked stunned.

Finally, Agent Sydney said, "OK, let me have the tablet, please. We're going to verify that. We'll look into the website and the emails. For the moment, we need you to stay in here. We'll have an agent outside the door, for your protection."

Colin tried hard not to roll his eyes. Yeah. Their protection.

The FBI agents, Len Steinberg, and the rest of the people got up to leave. Agent McElroy crouched down in front of Izzy. "Sweetie, can you tell us parents' phone number?" asked McElroy. "We can get them to come pick you up."

Colin saw Ana's hand tighten on Izzy's shoulder.

"No, thank you," said Izzy. "I'm staying with my sister."

The agents looked at each other, and Agent Sydney nodded. A moment later, the five of them were alone in the conference room.

"Good work, gang," said James dryly.

They all managed to smile.

* * *

"In the twenty-five years of my career, I've never seen anything like this," said Agent McElroy an hour later. "But it looks as if your story checks out."

Colin felt as if a physical weight had lifted off his chest. The others swapped relieved, disbelieving glances.

Maiv asked, "But how did you find out so quickly? The website, our emails . . . I was sure he would've scrubbed them by now."

Agent Sydney explained, "The FBI has actually been monitoring Huffmann for several months. It seems he was doing some insider trading while he . . ."

Colin finished, "Was masterminding an evil plan?"

"Apparently," said Agent McElroy without missing a beat. "Since we've already been tracking him, we were able to dig up the emails and website files pretty easily. He wasn't even trying to hide what he was doing on his own computer. It looks like he was that arrogant. And really, he could have been. The team watching him was looking specifically for insider trading, so none of this was on their radar. Anyway, we have it all."

Agent Sydney continued, "We will be bringing Huffmann into custody in about . . ." She checked her watch. "Ten minutes."

"So does that mean you're not arresting *us*?" asked James. "Because that would be awesome."

Agent Sydney frowned. "It's up to SolarStar and EarthWatch whether to press charges for your role in the burglaries. But for now, you're free to go. Your parents are on their way—all except yours, Ana."

Ana said quickly, "They're not my parents. And they're probably in some trouble of their own right about now." She took a deep breath. "I think you'd better contact social services instead."

James reached over and squeezed her hand. She squeezed back. Colin was glad to see how close they'd gotten. At least something good was coming out of the Contest.

"We'll look into that," Agent Sydney told Ana. "And we've gotten hold of Paul Grayson as well. He seems willing to cooperate."

"Oh sure, *now* he wants to be helpful," grumbled Colin. Maiv snorted.

"There's still one problem," Agent McElroy went on. "Huffmann clearly had help with setting up this 'contest,' as he called it. It seems that he hired someone else to do most of the bugging and hacking."

"And to kill us," added Colin. In his opinion, that part was pretty crucial.

"Possibly," said Agent McElroy, who clearly still wasn't quite sold. "We've recovered communication between Huffmann and this other person, but we haven't been able to track him down yet."

Maiv sat up straight. "You know, I think we can help with that."

* * *

At exactly 5:00 p.m., a man with a hat pulled low over his head walked to a garbage can on Nicollet Mall.

At 5:01, FBI agents surrounded him and arrested him.

At 5:22, as Colin sat with the others in the

SolarStar conference room, he heard a familiar voice behind him.

"Hey, loser. So they finally caught you?"

Danni stood at the door with their mom. With them stood a woman who had to be James's aunt, plus Maiv's whole family. In two seconds the room was filled with laughing, crying, hugging, and—in the case of Colin and his sister—some light punching.

Once again, everyone demanded answers. Colin knew it would take a long time to explain everything, but he finally felt strong enough to tell the story.

CHAPTER 16

MAIV

Maiv's mom kissed her face. Her dad squeezed her tight, and she felt the twins' little arms wrap around her. Over her dad's shoulder, she saw Colin being embraced by his mother and sister. James and his aunt leaned on each other and cried.

Ana and Izzy stood apart, hugging only each other. Then Maiv saw James reach out to Ana and bring the Rivera girls into his own small circle. Izzy threw her arms around James. Izzy really was the sweetest little girl.

Tears streamed from Maiv's eyes. She turned

back to her mom. "Niam, I only entered the Contest because I thought it could help you." Her mother squeezed her and whispered soft words. Soft words that said she was forgiven.

Maiv felt so tired she thought she might faint. "Can we go home, Niam?"

Before her mom could answer, a well-dressed white woman rushed into the conference room. She said to Agent Sydney, "These are the kids?" The FBI agent nodded.

The woman raised her voice to speak to the whole room. "James, Ana, Colin, Maiv—I'm Corinne Huffmann, the CEO of Huffmann Industries. I've just been informed of what's happened. I want to say how sorry I am. My father and I aren't on good terms, but this—"

For a moment she seemed at a loss for words. Then she pulled herself together and continued. "It's beyond anything I expected of him. I'm horrified. I know you all want to go home. So I'll make this brief. I've spoken to the executives of SolarStar and EarthWatch, and not only will they not press charges against the four of you, but in fact they consider you heroes. Because of you, their project can move forward. You probably already know by now that we're working on a completely solar-powered car that's more affordable and efficient than anything else on the market. You may have saved more than just a few companies."

She smiled, and Maiv felt a tiny surge of excitement. The project wasn't ruined.

Corinne continued, "And Huffmann Industries is equally grateful to you. I want to compensate you for what my father put you through—and reward you for your courage. Our charity foundation will be setting up a scholarship fund for each of you. You'll each be awarded $10 million, to be paid immediately."

CHAPTER 17
JAMES

Corinne Huffmann's announcement wasn't really sinking in. James felt as if he had a concussion. Ms. Huffmann started walking around the room, shaking hands and looking deeply into people's eyes. When she got to James, he thought, *She'd probably make a good politician.* He was grateful, of course. How could he not be? Her generosity was unbelievable. And apparently it was real, unlike her dad's. Still . . . there were some things this rich lady couldn't fix.

Aunt Beth put her arm around him. "Darling, let's go home."

James nodded.

It was time to say good-bye to his grandfather.

But first he turned to Ana and Izzy. "High five for the champion unicorn-drawer," he said to Izzy. She grinned slapped his outstretched palm with hers. "It was an honor to hang out with you, Isabel Rivera."

"The honor was ours, James Trudeleau," said Ana solemnly.

James looked up at her. "Where do you go now?"

Ana shrugged. "Another foster family. I've got evidence that Philip was abusing us. They'll send us somewhere else. Maybe split us up. But it's less than a year till I turn eighteen, and then I'll have this money and get Izzy back."

James said, "I can't believe this is real."

Just then, Colin came over to them. "I know, right? I guess I'll believe it when the money is in my bank account. This means my family can rebuild the store."

"I'm so glad!" said Ana. "I never would've forgiven myself if you'd lost the business."

Colin lowered his voice. "And Danni can

have her surgery too. If I can convince her to take a loan from me, anyway." He smiled over at his sister.

Maiv joined them too. "James, I meant to ask—how's your grandfather?"

James looked down. "He's fading. All the money in the world probably wouldn't save him. I have to go see him now. There's not much time left."

Izzy embraced him, and the other three piled on in an awkward, messy group hug. James sensed that they were all crying, though he couldn't see much through his own tears.

Nothing would ever be the same again. Nothing would take the place of his grandpa. But at least he had these people, these friends, in his life. "My grandpa would have liked you guys," he said.

Maiv pulled back and said in a choked voice, "James, call us, please. Let us know how you're doing."

Colin said, "Yeah, man. I mean, we'll see you at Huffmann's trial for sure, but that could be a zillion years from now. Stay in touch."

"Please do," Ana added and kissed his cheek.

James felt their support flow through him. "I will. And I've still got Colin's insurance papers and Ana's backpack, so stop by my apartment anytime."

Colin grinned. "Definitely."

Ana added, "Thank you, James, for everything."

"I wish we hadn't met this way," James said to all of them, "but I *am* glad we met."

As he and his aunt turned to leave, James knew that he was ready. He would be there for his grandpa, for however long they had left. And he would be the man his grandpa had believed he could be. He would make his grandpa proud.

James let out a long breath.

The Contest was over.

OCEAN COUNTY

ABOUT THE AUTHOR

Megan Atwood lives and works in Minneapolis, Minnesota, where she teaches creative writing at a local college and the Loft Literary Center. She has an MFA in writing for children and young adults and was a 2009 Artist Initiative grant recipient through the Minnesota State Arts Board. She has been published in literary and academic journals and has the best cat that has ever lived.

JAN   2016

JACKSON TOWNSHIP BRANCH
...ny Library
...27